Parent's Introduction

Whether your child is a beginning reader, a reluctant reader, or an eager reader, this book offers a fun and easy way to encourage and help your child in reading.

Developed with reading education specialists, *We Both Read* books invite you and your child to take turns reading aloud. You read the left-hand pages of the book, and your child reads the right-hand pages—which have been written at one of six early reading levels. The result is a wonderful new reading experience and faster reading development!

You may find it helpful to read the entire book aloud yourself the first time, then invite your child to participate the second time. As you read, try to make the story come alive by reading with expression. This will help to model good fluency. It will also be helpful to stop at various points to discuss what you are reading. This will help increase your child's understanding of what is being read.

In some books, a few challenging words are introduced in the parent's text, distinguished with **bold** lettering. Pointing out and discussing these words can help to build your child's reading vocabulary. If your child is a beginning reader, it may be helpful to run a finger under the text as each of you reads. Please also notice that a "talking parent" ☺ icon precedes the parent's text, and a "talking child" ☺ icon precedes the child's text.

If your child struggles with a word, you can encourage "sounding it out," but keep in mind that not all words can be sounded out. Your child might pick up clues about a word from the picture, other words in the sentence, or any rhyming patterns. If your child struggles with a word for more than five seconds, it is usually best to simply say the word.

Most of all, remember to praise your child's efforts and keep the reading fun. After you have finished the book, ask a few questions and discuss what you have read together. Rereading this book multiple times may also be helpful for your child.

Try to keep the tips above in mind as you read together, but don't worry about doing everything right. Simply sharing the enjoyment of reading together will increase your child's reading skills and help to start your child off on a lifetime of reading enjoyment!

Ben and Becky Get a Pet
We Both Read® Book

Text Copyright © 2018, 1998 by Sindy McKay
Illustrations Copyright © 1998 by Meredith Johnson

We Both Read® is a trademark of Treasure Bay, Inc.

Published by Treasure Bay, Inc.
P.O. Box 119
Novato, CA 94948 USA

Printed in Malaysia

Library of Congress Catalog Card Number: 98-60704

ISBN: 978-1-891327-10-0

We Both Read® Books

Visit us online at:
TreasureBayBooks.com

PR-11-19

We Both Read®

Ben and Becky Get a Pet

By Sindy McKay

Illustrated by Meredith Johnson

TREASURE BAY

This is a picture of my big sister and me.

My sister's name is Rebecca Elizabeth, but everyone calls her Becky. My mom says Becky is very strong-willed. I say, if there's something she wants, she usually gets it.

My name is Benjamin, but you can call me Ben.

Sometimes Becky and I get along. A lot of the time we don't. But one time Becky and I wanted the same thing, and we worked together to get it.

Becky and I wanted a pet.

We asked our mom about it, but she said it was up to our dad. So Becky and I pestered him about getting a pet for almost a month.

Mom said she'd never seen two kids who were more **persistent**.

I'm pretty sure **"persistent"** is a good thing.

I told Dad I wanted a snake named Killer. Becky said she wanted a kitten named Cupcake.

Dad said we would be lucky to get a pet at all.

5

"A pet is a big responsibility," he said. "Can you two be responsible?"

I crossed-my-heart-and-hoped-to-die that I could. Becky said that she was *always* **responsible**.

We could tell that Dad was beginning to soften, so we started begging really hard, "Please, oh please, oh please?"

"Okay," said Dad. "If you both think you can be **responsible** and take good care of it, I will let you get a pet."

"YES!!!" Becky and I were so happy that we hugged, but just for a second.

Dad, Becky, and I headed for the mall. I said I was going to get the biggest, meanest-looking snake in the world! Becky said that was never going to happen. She said I wouldn't even want a snake after I saw the sweet little kittens the animal rescue people had brought in.

The mall security **guard** held the door open for us.

Becky and I raced inside. The mall was full of people, but that didn't slow us down! We ran to the pet store as fast as we could. The **guard** ran after us and told us to slow down.

We dashed into the pet store and there, inside a big glass terrarium, was the greenest, shiniest snake I'd ever seen! A real "Killer"!

I lifted him out and felt his smooth, dry skin. He wasn't at all **slimy** like I thought he would be.

10

Becky was in another part of the store, looking at the kittens. I took Killer over to show her.

"Gross!" she said. "Why do you want a **slimy** old snake?"

I stuck Killer in her face and she screamed!

That's why I want a snake.

11

Becky ran off to tattle to Dad.

"Da-ad! Ben wants a slimy snake. Please inform him we are getting a fluffy kitten."

I held Killer up to Dad. "Admit it, Dad! This snake is **awesome**!" Killer's tongue darted out to say hello, then he began to **slither** up my arm to curl around my shoulder.

Dad had to admit it—Killer was cool.

"But," he said, "this pet is for both of you. Your sister has to like it too."

I tried to show Becky how **awesome** Killer was, but she said that a kitten that purrs is better than a snake that **slithers**.

Dad said, "I have to run some errands in the mall. You two stay here and make a decision about your pet." Then he left, reminding us to stay together and not to fight.

I looked at the amazing snake on my **shoulder** and decided there was only one thing to do.

I had to make Becky see how great Killer was.

"Killer is so cool," I told her. "His skin comes off. He has no ears. He eats rats. He's great. He's wonderful! He's awesome!!"

Becky pointed to my **shoulder** and said, "He's gone."

15

It was true! Killer had slithered off my shoulder and disappeared. Becky and I **searched** the store, but we couldn't find him anywhere!

Becky was so mad her eyes almost popped out of her head. "Ben, you are sooo irresponsible! Now Dad is never going to let us get a pet."

Becky was right. We had to find Killer or Dad would not let us get any pet.

I started to **search** the store again. I just had to find him!

Suddenly Becky screamed and pointed toward the wall. "There he is, Ben! Stop him before he gets away!"

I wasn't worried. After all, not even a snake can go through a wall. Unless, of course, there's a *hole* in the wall. Before I could stop him, Killer slipped into the hole and disappeared.

"Great," said Becky. "Now we'll *never* find him!"
"Yes, we will," I said. But I didn't know how.
Suddenly we heard a scream from the music shop next door. I smiled at Becky. "See? I told you we would find him."

Becky and I raced next door and found a saleslady standing on top of the counter, screaming. She stopped screaming for a moment to politely ask, "May I help you?" We told her we were looking for a snake and she pointed at Killer. Then she started to scream again.

I told Becky to stay by the door so he couldn't get
away. Then I ran over to grab him.

I missed.

Killer headed for the door at supersonic speed!
I yelled for Becky to grab him, but she yelled back
that she wouldn't even *touch* a snake.

Besides, Becky was nowhere near the door anymore. She was on top of the counter with the saleslady, and they were both screaming their guts out!

I ran out the door after Killer.

I saw him slither his way into a candy store. I started to run in after him. Suddenly Becky pushed me to the ground.

She slapped her hand over my mouth and pointed. Inside the candy store was the security guard and inside a jar of candy sticks was Killer.

We held our breaths as the guard started to reach for a candy stick. We let out a sigh of relief when he decided to take a jawbreaker instead.

The guard left and I shouted, "Quick, Becky! Grab Killer!"

Becky shouted back, "Are you crazy? I will never grab a slimy snake!"

While we were fighting, Killer went back out into the mall.

Becky and I ran after him, dodging and weaving through people as we searched the crowded mall.

I bumped into a guy with a hot dog and totally freaked when I saw his hot dog moving! Then I **realized** it was not a hot dog. It was Killer.

The man **realized** it too. He threw his hot dog bun into the air. It came down on top of a lady's head. Killer crawled out of the bun and began to slither down her neck.

Boy, did she scream!

Now everyone knew there was a snake in the mall and things went totally crazy.

People ran into stores! Out to their cars! Up onto benches! Into the trash cans! Becky said it was "mass hysteria."

And it was all because of a little green snake.

Becky and I looked around. The crowd was gone now—except for the people in the trash cans. It should have been easy to find Killer.

It *should* have been, but it wasn't.

"Let's just forget it, Becky. We're never going to find him."

"Don't worry. We're going to find him," Becky said. "And that disgusting snake is not going to escape again."

"But how will we find him?"

Becky said all we had to do was listen.

Becky was right because just then we heard a shriek. It came from the dress shop across the way.

A screaming lady ran out of the door. Becky and I ran in to look for Killer.

I spotted Killer scooting under a dressing room door so I scooted in after him. Inside a lady was putting on a belt— only it wasn't really a belt she was putting on. It was Killer. I was so excited I shouted, "There's my *snake*!" The woman screamed and dropped Killer.

I grabbed for him, but someone grabbed me first.
It was the security guard.

"You're in big trouble, young man."

He said it wasn't nice to scare people by saying
there was a snake in the store. I told him there really
was a snake, but I don't think he believed me.

The guard was taking me to his security station when Becky ran up and tried to explain things. He didn't believe her either. The only way to make him believe us was to show him the snake. To do that, Becky had to catch Killer.

The guard was right. I was in big trouble.

"Don't worry," said Becky. "I'm going to catch that sneaky, slimy snake. I won't like it, but I'll do it!" And off she ran to find Killer.

This would be the hardest thing Becky would ever do.

Becky told me later that it took every ounce of courage in her whole entire body to pick up Killer, but she was surprised when she felt his smooth, cool skin. He wrapped himself around her arm and she raced through the mall to show him to the security guard.

Boy, was I happy to see Becky and that snake! She held him up to the security guard's face. "See?" she said. "There really was a snake."

The guard took one look at Killer and fainted. I think he finally believed us.

"Let's not tell Dad about this," Becky suggested as we hurried back to the pet store. "No need to upset him."

But we did tell Dad about it. All of it. And we admitted that a pet was a pretty big responsibility—one that maybe we weren't ready for yet.

We waited for Dad to yell at us, but he didn't yell. He smiled! "A big pet can be a lot of work," he said. "So why don't we start out small."

Then he took something from behind his back.

 "Oh, my gosh, it's a **hamster**," Becky squealed as she took the little fur ball from Dad. "He's the cutest little thing in the whole entire world!"

"He's not cute," I said. "He's a Killer!"

And that's the story of how my sister and I got a pet.

As we left the mall with our new **hamster**, we saw the security guard. I told him I was sorry about what happened with the old Killer. I asked him if he wanted to meet the new Killer, but he said, "NO THANKS!"
I wonder why.

If you liked *Ben and Becky Get a Pet,* here are some other

We Both Read books you are sure to enjoy!

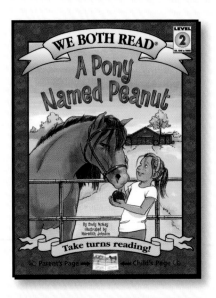

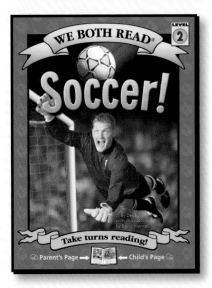